Primary Sources of Colonial America

The French and Indian War

Gerry Boehme

Cavendish Square
New York

Published in 2018 by Cavendish Square Publishing, LLC
243 5th Avenue, Suite 136, New York, NY 10016

First Edition

Library of Congress Cataloging-in-Publication Data

Names: Boehme, Gerry, author.
Title: The French and Indian War / Gerry Boehme.
Description: New York : Cavendish Square Publishing, 2018. | Series: Primary sources of colonial America | Includes bibliographical references and index.
Identifiers: LCCN 2017019290 (print) | LCCN 2017020165 (ebook) | ISBN 9781502631459 (E-book) | ISBN 9781502631442 (library bound)| ISBN 9781502634597 (pbk.)
Subjects: LCSH: United States--History--French and Indian War, 1754-1763--Juvenile literature.
Classification: LCC E199 (ebook) | LCC E199 .B666 2018 (print) | DDC 940.2/534--dc23
LC record available at https://lccn.loc.gov/2017019290

Editorial Director: David McNamara
Editor: Fletcher Doyle
Copy Editor: Rebecca Rohan
Associate Art Director: Amy Greenan
Designer: Lindsey Auten
Production Coordinator: Karol Szymczuk
Photo Research: J8 Media

The photographs in this book are used by permission and through the courtesy of: Photos credits: Cover Photo Researchers/Science History Images/Alamy Stock Photo; p. 5 Buyenlarge/Archive Photos/Getty Images; p. 6 Andriy Blokhin/Shutterstock.com; p. 9 David Monniaux/Wikimedia Commons/File:Claude Bernou Carte de 1Amerique septentrionale.jpg/CC PD; p. 12 Archive Photos/Getty Images; p. 14 Sue Smith/Shutterstock.com; p. 16, 45 North Wind Picture Archives/Alamy Stock Photo; p. 18 Jeffrey M. Frank/Shutterstock.com; p. 25 Peter Newark American Pictures/Bridgeman Images; p. 31 Chicago History Museum, USA/Bridgeman Images; p. 33 Albert Bobbett/Library of Congress; p. 35 Hoodinski/Wikimedia Commons/File:French and Indian war map.svg/CC BY-SA 3.0; p. 38 Bettmann/Getty Images; p. 41 John Gibson, New York Public Library/Wikimedia Commons/File:The British governments in Nth. America-laid down agreeable to the proclamation of Octr. 7, 1763 NYPL435005.tiff/CC PD; p. 43 Everett – Art/Shutterstock.com; p. 47 Victorian Traditions/Shutterstock.com; p. 49 Interim Archives/Getty Images.

Printed in the United States of America

CONTENTS

INTRODUCTION

The War That Shaped America

In 1823, American author James Fenimore Cooper wrote a book he titled *The Pioneer.* It was the first of what turned out to be five novels in a series that came to be known as *The Leatherstocking Tales*. Cooper published his most famous book, *The Last of the Mohicans*, in 1826. People still read his novel today, and it has been made into several movies, including an award-winning version watched by millions since it debuted in 1992.

Set in the North American wilderness of the 1700s, *The Last of the Mohicans* dramatically portrays the hardships of life in colonial times. The European powers of France and England had been fighting for centuries over land, wealth, and power. Beginning in 1689, these European wars spread to involve the colonies that Europe had established in the New World.

Over the next seventy years, France and England would battle for control of North America. The last of these wars, the French and Indian War of 1754–1763, determined the fate of the North American continent.

Before the French and Indian War, French and English colonists often coexisted with Native Americans in the wilderness of North America.

Unlike previous conflicts between Great Britain and France, this war actually started in North America in 1754 before it spread in 1756 to Europe and the rest of the world, where it was called the Seven Years' War. Historians consider the French and Indian War to be the first world war.

Why That Name?

The name we use to describe this great conflict can be confusing, however, since it was not fought between the French and Native Americans (who were called Indians in those days). The British looked at the war as something they fought against the French and Native Americans, so they called it the French and Indian War. They then passed that title down to us.

France, however, uses a different name. French people who lived in Canada referred to the war as the *Guerre de la Conquête* (War of Conquest) since they viewed the British as conquerors who took over their land.

When the fighting finally ended, England had won all of France's former territory on the continent, including land

Streets in New Orleans still carry names given by early French settlers. French heritage lives on in the United States and Canada.

west of the Appalachian Mountains and all of Canada. When England tried to manage its new empire, however, some of its decisions made its colonists very angry. Eventually, the colonists' rage grew into a strong desire for freedom.

Less than fifteen years after the French and Indian War ended, the American colonies declared their independence from Great Britain, and the Revolutionary War began.

The French and Indian War had other major effects as well. Its savage battles helped to increase the level of mistrust between white settlers and Native Americans. George Washington commanded troops for the first time and learned about new **tactics** that would help him lead the Continental Army during the American Revolution.

Today, the US city of New Orleans still boasts of its French Quarter, and French settlers expelled from Canada became the Cajuns of Louisiana. And, while citizens of Canada primarily speak English, French remains the official language in the province of Quebec.

The French and Indian War shaped an entire continent and led directly to the founding of the United States.

CHAPTER ONE

Setting the Stage

When Christopher Columbus first set foot on a small island in the Bahamas in 1492, few people could have predicted that his voyage would eventually change life for millions of people around the world. Over the next three hundred years, the great powers of Europe would begin to explore and settle the strange and mysterious lands they called the New World. These territories included the continents of North and South America, as well as Central America and the islands of the Caribbean Sea.

Power and Wealth

The explorers who were sent to the New World by their European kings and queens returned with tales of limitless natural resources just waiting to be collected and brought back to the home country. Some reported great amounts of minerals like gold and silver. Others spoke of teeming numbers of animals and fish that could clothe and feed their nations. Still more described fertile soil that could support farms and permanent settlements.

Always looking for new sources of power and wealth, the countries of western Europe quickly acted to send more explorers and early settlers to claim parts of these new territories for their home countries. These nations included Great Britain (England, Scotland, Ireland and Wales), France, Spain, Portugal, and the Netherlands (the home of the Dutch people).

The Competition Begins

In time, each European nation began to concentrate on different territories in the Americas. Portugal centered its attention on South America, especially Brazil. The Dutch built a series of trading posts, towns, and forts up and down the Hudson River from present-day New York to Albany. Spain's holdings were much more extensive, including Central and South America, the West Indies, Mexico, and what we know today as Florida and the southwestern United States.

France and England, on the other hand, focused almost all their attention on North America.

France and England

In 1534, navigator Jacques Cartier claimed northern North America for France and gave the name New France to the area around the St. Lawrence River. In 1608, Samuel de Champlain founded Quebec in what is now Canada. Champlain also explored the Great Lakes and Hudson Bay, and eventually made it to the Mississippi River.

The British established their first successful permanent settlement in Jamestown, Virginia in 1607. Within ten years, English settlements stretched along the shores of Chesapeake Bay. Eventually, Great Britain claimed all the land along the coast of the Atlantic Ocean that stretched from Maine south to Georgia and west to the Appalachian Mountains.

This French map from the 1680s shows the locations of French, British, and Spanish land claims in North, Central, and parts of South America.

Some Europeans came to the New World looking for adventure and wealth, but others hoped to find a better life and personal freedom. For example, the Pilgrims did not follow the Anglican Church, the official faith of the Church of England headed by the King. They came to North America looking for religious freedom and settled in the Plymouth colony in Massachusetts.

Rivalry

By the early 1700s, England and France were left to fight over control of North America. The Dutch had lost their territory to the British. Spain had decided that, aside from the remaining settlements in Florida, it would concentrate on New Spain (what is now Mexico).

The boundaries between the French and British colonies ran along the northern and western borders of New England, New York, Pennsylvania, and Virginia. French territory stretched from Canada across the Great Lakes and along the Mississippi River to New Orleans in modern-day Louisiana. The British settled in colonies along the East Coast, but they wanted to move west to control even more land.

While both England and France wanted to run North America, the countries had very different reasons for going there.

Furs and Water

The French came looking for new trading opportunities. They discovered that the abundant wildlife could supply valuable **pelts** to make clothing and hats that were in great demand in Europe. They saw North America as one big fur trading empire, and they wanted to take control of the long rivers and large lakes in the area.

Back then, North America was mostly covered with forests and mountains, which made travel over land slow and dangerous. The easiest way to move about was by boat. The French wanted to use the waterways of the Great Lakes and big rivers like the Ohio and the Mississippi to transport their goods. The lakes and rivers also connected French territories in Canada to their other lands in Illinois and Louisiana to the south and west.

Farms and Homes

Great Britain had a different plan. England wanted its people to move to the colonies to transform the land and make permanent settlements. As the colonies became more successful, they could send money and goods back to the home country.

Some colonists were tradesman and fishermen, and they built towns and small cities. Others were farmers, and as more settlers came from Great Britain they needed more farmland. The population grew, and colonies like Pennsylvania and Virginia hoped to expand to new territory to the west.

By the mid-1700s, the British colonial population in North American was about twenty times larger than the French. Some estimates say that British colonists numbered more than two hundred thousand, while the French only had ten thousand. However, the French and English populations were still very small compared to another group of people who had lived in these areas hundreds of years before the European colonists arrived.

Native Americans Already Here

When Columbus first landed in the Caribbean, he thought he had arrived in India, so he called the native people he met Indians. Even though the Europeans soon discovered their mistake, they continued to refer to the **indigenous** people that way.

Millions of Native Americans lived in North America when the first European settlers arrived. While no one knows for sure, there were probably about three hundred thousand Native Americans living near the areas where the British and French were settling.

Most of the Native Americans who lived in the northeast portion of the continent belonged to one of two large groups. The Algonquin tribe lived in Southern Quebec and Eastern Ontario in Canada. They spoke a version of the Algonquian language. So did dozens of other tribes that were spread over a wide area that included the Great Lakes as well as the Atlantic Coast.

Another even stronger group was the Iroquois **Confederacy** of the Onondaga, Oneida, Seneca, Cayuga,

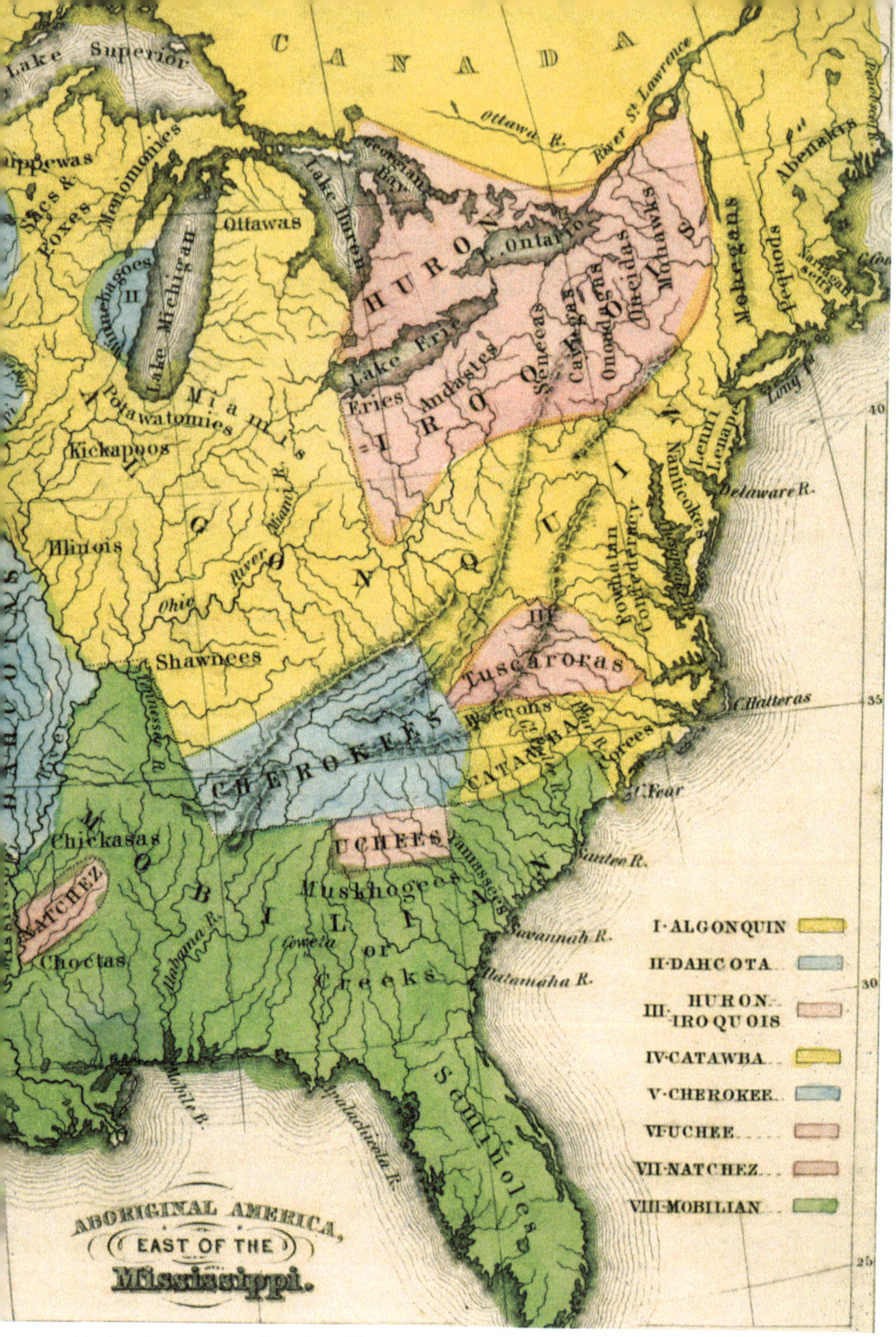

Native American tribes lived for hundreds of years in North America before European settlers arrived. This early map shows the locations of major tribes.

Mohawk, and Tuscarora peoples. These tribes had decided to form an **alliance** for their common protection, and their union commanded fear and respect from the Algonquian-speaking tribes as well as the European colonists who lived in the area. Most of the Iroquois tribes lived in the region we know today as New York State.

Both the Iroquois and the Algonquian speakers supported themselves by hunting, fishing, farming, and trading. Their families lived in large communities. Women played an important role in tribal leadership and in raising crops.

Trade and Guns

The first meetings between Native Americans and Europeans were often friendly. In fact, some early settlers only managed to survive their first years in the harsh North American winters due to help they received from the Native Americans who already lived there.

Native Americans had always traded with each other in order to get the things they needed. The newly arrived Europeans brought many new goods to trade, including metal pots, tools, cloth, and blankets. The Europeans also introduced the native peoples to advanced weapons, including muskets and pistols. These weapons were vastly superior to the bows and arrows and **tomahawks** that the tribes had been using for hunting and warfare.

Caught Up

Aside from the Iroquois, most Native American tribes did not look at themselves as one united people. They saw themselves as separate tribes that needed to look out for their own interests. As they became more dependent on the guns and other goods they received from Europeans in return for their pelts, Native Americans got more involved in the wars that their new European partners were fighting against each other.

Sir William Johnson: Colonist and Native American Ally

William Johnson was born in 1715 in Ireland. He came to North America in 1738 and built a trading post near Schenectady, New York. Johnson became friends with the Mohawks and other tribes that lived in the area. He learned their languages, dressed in their clothing, and helped them receive an education.

Some colonists did not understand why Johnson was so comfortable with Native Americans. One Englishman wrote that Johnson was "continually plagued with Indians about him" and that they "spoil his garden and keep his house always dirty."

William Johnson's gravesite depicts his friendship with Native Americans.

However, Native Americans respected Johnson and trusted him. They said, "He speaks with a straight tongue," and they gave him the name "Warraghiyagey," which meant "one who does much business." His last wife, Molly Brant, was the sister of the Mohawk leader Joseph Brant.

Johnson gained fame during the French and Indian War as a military leader and by convincing many tribes, especially the Iroquois, to help England against France.

In many cases, Native Americans decided to join with their white trading partners to gain an advantage or to settle old scores against other tribes. They also looked to Europeans to help protect their territory.

Coexist or Compete

The different plans that France and England had for their colonies led them to treat Native Americans differently as well.

French explorers, traders, and missionaries lived alongside Native Americans. French missionaries tried to convert Native peoples to Catholicism. The French built forts and trading posts near major rivers and formed alliances with Native American tribes in each area. These tribes included the Algonquin, Delaware, Ojibwa, Shawnee, Potawatomi, Ottawa, and Menominee.

Many of these tribes still fought against each other, but they all hated the Iroquois even more. The French encouraged these tribes to attack the British and their Iroquois allies.

The English were also interested in trading with Native American tribes. The Dutch had formed valuable trading relationships with the Iroquois. When the British took control of the former Dutch territories, they built their own connections. The British also encouraged the Iroquois to attack Algonquin tribes to their north, as well as the Algonquian-speaking allies and the French themselves.

Conflicts Over Land

The English colonies were interested in trade, but their main goal was to expand their settlements. Most Native tribes felt more threatened by the English than by the French. The English insisted on moving onto lands that Native Americans had lived on for hundreds of years.

An Iroquois leader named Cannasatego gave a speech during the early 1740s in which he told English colonists to stay off Native American land:

English colonists sold captured Native Americans into slavery, inspiring even more bitterness among native tribes and pushing many to support the French.

> We know our lands are now become more valuable … Your people daily settle on these lands, and spoil our hunting. … we now renew our request [to]inform the … people are seated on our lands, that that country belongs to us, in right of conquest; we having bought it with our blood, and taken it from our enemies in fair war. …

In New England in particular, English settlers and Native Americans waged bloody fights over land, leading to misery and death for both sides.

Slave Trade

The English also brought African slaves to North America. By 1700, there were about twenty-eight thousand African slaves in the American colonies. The English were always looking for more slaves to work on their plantations in the South, however, and they began to pay their Native American allies to capture enemies from other tribes and sell them into slavery.

This cruel practice caused many Native American tribes to hate the English settlers even more and convinced them to ask the French for help against these British invaders and slave traders.

With France and England at each others' throats, and with Native Americans forced to choose sides between the two European powers, the stage had been set for a series of savage conflicts that would change the face of North America.

The French and Indian War was about to begin.

DEH-GE-WA-NUS

CHAPTER TWO

The Path to War

France and England had long been bitter rivals. They had fought in Europe over wealth and territory for hundreds of years. When European kings and queens sent explorers and settlers to foreign lands, they still considered the colonists to be their citizens. So, when wars broke out in Europe, rulers expected colonists to prove their loyalty and fight the same enemies where they lived.

As the colonies grew, it was no surprise that wars in Europe began to spill over to North America. They truly were becoming world wars. Unfortunately, these wars did not just involve soldiers. Unlike most European battles, the fighting in North America included savage attacks on civilians as well, including women and children.

Mary Jemison was one of many white settlers captured by Native Americans. She chose to live with a Seneca tribe in Western New York.

Three Wars

Beginning in 1689, England and France fought three different wars that extended to their colonies in North America. British settlers named each war after their King or Queen who ruled at the time: King William's War (1689–1697), Queen Anne's War (1702–1713), and King George's War (1744–1748).

During King William's War, the Governor of New France ordered his forces to attack English towns in New York and New England. On a cold winter night in 1690, the French and their Algonquian-speaking allies crossed the frozen ice of Lake Champlain to attack the small English settlement of Schenectady, New York, massacring many settlers and kidnapping many others.

Meaningless Suffering

The English colonies and their Iroquois allies fought back, and the next few years featured a series of cruel battles. When England and France finally signed a peace treaty in 1697, they forced their colonies to return all the land they'd captured to the other side. For the French and the English colonists, all the death, destruction, and suffering had meant nothing.

Just four years later, Queen Anne's War broke out in Europe, and it spread to North America in 1702. Civilians again became targets of brutal attacks by both sides. Torture and **scalping** were commonplace, and women and children were just as likely to be slaughtered as soldiers and the men who lived in the villages.

When this war ended in 1713, the French were forced to give some of their territory to Great Britain, but the bloodshed between France and England was far from over.

King George's War began in 1744, and settlements along the border were once more subjected to terrible attacks. In one of the major battles, the English successfully captured the French fortress of Louisbourg after a six-week **siege**.

Captured

Settlers endured great suffering during the years of war between England and France. Many who escaped death were taken prisoner by Native American fighters.

On April 5, 1758, fifteen-year-old Mary Jemison and her family were captured by the Shawnee. In 1824, she recalled what happened:

> When we set off, an Indian in the forward canoe took the scalps of my former friends, strung them on a pole that he placed upon his shoulder … On the way we passed a Shawnee town, where I saw a number of heads, arms, legs, and other fragments of the bodies of some white people who had just been burned.
>
> All the prisoners [are given] to the bereaved [Native American] families … It was my happy lot to be accepted for adoption. … I was received by the two squaws to [a brother who had been killed], and I was … treated by them as a real sister, the same as though I had been born of their mother.

Mary chose to live with the tribe until she died in 1833 at age ninety-one. There is a statue of her in Letchworth State Park, near where she lived in New York State.

Louisbourg was very important, since it controlled the entrance to the St. Lawrence River and all of Canada. Just imagine how angry the English colonists became when, in the latest peace treaty, the English government traded Louisbourg back to the French in return for territory in far-away India!

Lingering Resentment

The Treaty of Aix-la-Chapelle, which ended King George's War, also established clear borders between the French and British colonies in North America.

However, neither French nor English settlers were happy with the borders that their leaders had agreed to thousands of miles away. Both sides had suffered during the three wars, and they felt bitter over returning land that they had fought and died for. The seeds had already been planted for an even larger conflict soon to occur.

Those seeds would take root in territory located west of the Appalachian Mountains and north of the Ohio River. The rich lands known as the Ohio country would set the stage for the bloody fight known as the French and Indian War.

The Fight for Ohio

The Ohio country covered an area from Upper Louisiana all the way to Canada. It was rich in natural resources, including timber, minerals, and fur-bearing animals. The Ohio River also provided the fastest way to travel through the interior of North America.

For the French, the river and its surrounding territory could provide more animals for the fur trade as well as an easy connection from its Canadian settlements to the Mississippi River and New Orleans. The French began to worry that English colonies might expand and threaten their water routes, so they began to build a series of forts from the Great Lakes to the Ohio River.

The English, on the other hand, saw the Ohio country as their chance to expand their colonies to the west in search of more farmland. The colony of Virginia had claimed the Ohio territory for itself and was determined to protect its interests.

France and England began a race to control the Ohio Valley. Both countries wanted to build forts in the area to prevent the other from taking over. A particularly important spot lay at the forks of the Ohio River, where the Allegheny, Monongahela, and Ohio Rivers meet—the site of modern-day Pittsburgh.

Enter George Washington

In 1753, Robert Dinwiddie, the governor of Virginia, sent a young **militia** officer and **surveyor** named George Washington to warn the French to leave the Ohio area. Dinwiddie ordered Washington to give a letter to the French commander. The letter read:

> Sir,
>
> The lands upon the River Ohio, in the western parts of the Colony of Virginia, are so notoriously known to be the property of the Crown of Great Britain that it is a matter of equal concern and surprise to me, to hear that a body of French forces are erecting fortresses and making settlements upon that river, within his Majesty's dominions.
>
> The many and repeated complaints I have received of these acts of hostility lay me under the necessity of sending, in the name of the King, my master, the bearer hereof, George Washington, Esq., one of the Adjutants-General of the forces of this dominion, to complain to you of the encroachments thus made, and of the injuries done to the subjects of Great Britain, in violation of the law of nations, and the treaties now subsisting between the two Crowns. If these facts be true, and you think fit to justify your

> proceedings, I must desire you to acquaint me by whose authority and instructions you have lately marched from Canada with an armed force, and invaded the King of Great Britain's territories.
>
> However, sir, in obedience to my instructions, it becomes my duty to require your peaceable departure; and that you would forbear prosecuting a purpose so interruptive of the harmony and good understanding, which his Majesty is desirous to continue and cultivate with the most Christian King.
>
> I flatter myself that you will be pleased to receive Major Washington with the evidences of courtesy and politeness which are natural to your nation, and I shall be at the height of satisfaction if you send him back with a reply conforming to my wishes for a durable peace between us.
>
> I have the honor to be,
> Sir,
> Your very humble,
> ROBERT DINWIDDIE.
>
> Williamsburg, in Virginia,
> October 31, 1753.

Dinwiddie's letter shows that, in those days, enemies communicated with each other in very polite language. The French understood his true meaning, however.

Virginia was claiming the lands by the Ohio River and telling the French to leave. The French totally ignored Dinwiddie's demands. The French commander reportedly replied, "I do not think myself obliged to obey it."

Governor Dinwiddie sent Washington and about 150 soldiers to reinforce British troops in the territory in 1754. When he arrived, Washington found that the French now

While serving in the Virginia militia, George Washington attempted to expel French forces from the Ohio territory.

controlled the area. Some Native American allies then reported that a small group of French soldiers had camped nearby and that they could be surprised.

First Shots Fired

On May 28, 1754, Washington led an attack on the French camp, killing the commander and twelve soldiers while taking others as prisoners. Washington, who would later lead the colonial army against the British in the American Revolution and then serve as the new nation's first president, had just fired the first shots of the French and Indian War.

Other French soldiers soon learned of Washington's assault and moved to confront the English. Washington built a small **stockade** near the forks of the Ohio that he named Fort Necessity. The French attacked with a larger force, however, and forced Washington to surrender. The French then allowed Washington and his men to head back to their homes in Virginia but gave them a warning to stay out of the Ohio Valley. Washington did, but not without first drawing maps of the region.

British colonists now feared more attacks by French forces. Seven of the thirteen colonies sent representatives to Albany, New York to discuss forming an alliance to defend themselves against possible French aggression. Benjamin Franklin of Pennsylvania proposed in his Albany Plan that the colonies actually unite under one president and a ruling council.

At that time, however, the colonies still considered themselves to be separate, and they did not want to cede any power to a central government. Some believe, however, that Franklin's proposal planted a seed. That seed would later grow into a full-fledged independence movement that would unite the colonies about twenty years later.

Native American Alliances

When hostilities once again broke out between the French and the British, the French convinced many Native American tribes that the British were threatening their lands and their independence. This helped the French expand their trade relationships into military alliances.

The British tried to do the same, but with less success. British colonists met with more than one hundred leaders of the Iroquois nations, who were very powerful at that time, in order to form an alliance against the French. The Iroquois did not trust the British, however, and all they would offer was a promise to remain **neutral**. Hendrick, a leader of the Mohawk tribe that was part of the Iroquois Confederacy, showed both his mistrust of the English and his fear of the consequences of war when he said to the colonists:

> The [British] neglected us for these three years past. You have thrown us behind your back whereas the French are a subtle and vigilant people, always using their utmost endeavors to seduce us and bring us over to them … The Governor of Virginia and the Governor of Canada are quarrelling about lands which belong to us, and their quarrel may end in our destruction.

The Fight Begins

The British decided that they needed to move the French out of the Ohio country. The French had built a new fort, Fort Duquesne, at the forks of the Ohio. In July 1755, the British sent a force under General Edward Braddock to attack the fort. George Washington served as one of Braddock's officers during the campaign.

The terrain that Braddock and the English army faced was much different than what they were used to in the battlefields of Europe. In his report about his march to Fort Duquesne, Braddock wrote, "I have an [sic] hundred and ten miles to march through an uninhabitable wilderness over steep and rocky mountains and almost impassible [swamp]."

In addition to the terrain, the British army was also not prepared for the way that the French had learned to fight in North America.

In Europe, opposing nations fought battles in open fields, using large armies, careful planning and slow, precise movements.

North America was different. The same conditions that made travel difficult, including heavy forests and impassable mountains, made it hard to coordinate large armies. This led soldiers to adopt new tactics in battle. The French had learned many new techniques from their Native American allies, who had been fighting other tribes in these lands for hundreds of years.

The French and their Native American allies used frontier warfare. They hid in the woods and launched surprise attacks. Rather than conduct long engagements with many soldiers, French fighters used quick, surprise strikes against the British, with many advances and withdrawals. Some called this **guerrilla warfare**.

Stubborn Leader

George Washington and others with experience fighting in North America tried to warn Braddock that wilderness fighting was different, but Braddock would not listen. He believed that his experienced British troops were superior to the English colonial fighters and that he would easily defeat the French and their Native American allies:

> These [French and Indians] may, indeed, be a formidable enemy to your raw American militia, but upon the king's regular and [disciplined] troops, sir, it is impossible they should make any impression.

The British force under Braddock numbered about 1,500 British soldiers and colonial militiamen. On July 9, 1755, they met a smaller force of French and Native Americans by the Monongahela River in what is today Pennsylvania. The results were disastrous for the British.

Battle of Monongahela

Braddock still expected the French to fight as they did in Europe, like gentlemen. As Washington had warned, however, the French hid in the woods and attacked. To make matters worse, the British used their traditional strategy of standing close together in the clearings surrounded by trees, and their bright red coats and close formations made them easy targets.

The British withdrew after suffering heavy losses, perhaps almost one thousand men. General Braddock later died from wounds he suffered during the battle. According to one British officer, the French and Native Americans:

> … pursued us butchering as they came as [far] as the other side of [the] river; during our crossing, they shot many in the Water, and dyed the stream with their blood, scalping and cutting them in a most barbarous manner. Hundreds of bodies littered the road, and every fallen British soldier was scalped and his body stripped.

According to Benjamin Franklin, Braddock admitted before he died that he used poor tactics in his fight, saying with his last words, "We shall better know how to deal with them another time."

The British defeat at the Battle of Monongahela, also known as the Battle of the Wilderness, convinced more Native American tribes to support the French. Unfortunately for the British, Monongahela turned out to be only the first in a string of costly losses for their forces.

CHAPTER THREE

Great Britain Triumphs

When the French defeated Washington at Fort Necessity, the government of Virginia asked Great Britain for help. At first, the British king refused. England had just ended a war with France six years earlier, and King George II wanted to avoid another fight. The British **prime minister** advised, "Let Americans fight Americans."

The king changed his mind, however, when it became clear that his colonies would probably lose to the French army if Great Britain did not send troops. King George ordered General Edward Braddock to go to Virginia and expel the French from Fort Duquesne and the Ohio country.

Early English Losses

Braddock's terrible defeat at Monongahela shocked Great Britain. Not only did the French use tactics that were more effective in the forests of North America, but they and their Native American allies had also built a larger and superior

British General Edward Braddock refused to adapt his battlefield tactics to wilderness fighting. His defeat at Monongahela left him mortally wounded.

fighting force. Over the next four years, France consistently defeated the British in battle after battle.

In one of their few victories, the English defeated a French force near Lake George on September 8, 1755. After their victory, the English built Fort William Henry on the southern end of the lake. In the meantime, the French constructed Fort Carillon at Ticonderoga, which was near the south shore of Lake Champlain and only about 35 miles (56 km) north.

In 1756, the French captured Fort Oswego on Lake Ontario in New York. The next year, French General Louis-Joseph de Montcalm-Grozon laid siege to Fort William Henry. When the British soldiers and their colonial militia finally surrendered, Montcalm permitted them to leave the fort and make their way to the nearest British lines.

Strange Rules

Even though Montcalm was now fighting in North America, he still followed some of the traditional European practices of waging war. When two sides battled, he believed, they were supposed to act like gentlemen. If the enemy army surrendered, the soldiers were often allowed to return home while keeping their weapons and possessions as long as they promised not to fight again.

However, Montcalm's Native American allies did not understand these foreign rules and were unhappy with the terms of the surrender. Native Americans did not fight for the pride of European countries or for a regular salary like the soldiers did. Instead, tribes usually received food or money from the French or British for their help.

Even more important, in their wars against other tribes, Native American warriors usually took valuables and other personal belongings from the people they killed in battle. They fully expected to get the same benefits when they helped beat the English at Fort William Henry, and they felt betrayed when the French let the Englishmen go and would not let the tribes collect their rewards.

Killing Spree

What happened next was a terrible **massacre** that historians still talk about today. Perhaps most famously, American author James Fenimore Cooper immortalized the story in his 1826 novel *The Last of the Mohicans*.

Montcalm's Native allies refused to honor the deal that Montcalm made with the British. When the English column abandoned Fort William Henry, they had to leave some of their wounded and other people behind. Native American warriors, including members of the Ottawa, Potawatomi, Abenaki, and Huron tribes, then forced their way into the fort. They stole clothing and other valuables from the helpless prisoners while killing and scalping many as well.

The tribes then chased after and attacked the British who had left. The English column did not just include soldiers and militia; women and children also lived at Fort William Henry or had gone there for protection.

Native warriors disobeyed their French allies and attacked English soldiers and settlers who had already surrendered at Fort William Henry.

Historical accounts differ about the carnage that followed. Some claim that thousands of English soldiers, militia, women, and children were slaughtered by the angry Native American tribes. Others believe that the casualties numbered in the hundreds, and that most of the English eventually made their way back safely.

Whether hundreds or thousands died, the attack made some things clear. The French were having more and more trouble controlling the behavior of their Native American allies due to their different languages and cultures. For their part, Native Americans began to lose trust in their white allies and, after taking Fort William Henry, they never fought again in such large numbers for the French.

On a broader scale, both the French and the British viewed Native Americans with more suspicion. Whites began to think of all tribes as enemies. This suspicion would turn into racial hatred, and that would affect relations between whites and Native Americans for hundreds of years afterward.

World War

By 1756, the war between England and France in North America had spread to Europe. The German states of Prussia and Hanover joined Great Britain, while Austria, Spain, and Russia joined France. The Seven Years' War, as it came to be known in Europe, now stretched from one side of the Atlantic to the other and included other distant colonies, including the West Indies, Africa, and India.

Spain tried to stay out of the war at first. As it progressed, however, the Spanish king began to fear that if Great Britain won, its growing power could hurt Spain's position in the Americas. After signing an agreement with France in 1761, Spain entered the Seven Years' War against Britain in 1762.

Turning the Tide

Experiencing crushing losses since the beginning of the war convinced the British they needed new leadership. They chose William Pitt to be their new prime minister in 1757. Pitt was very confident that he could defeat France both in North America and in Europe, saying, "I am sure I can save this country, and that nobody else can."

Pitt sent new generals and more troops to North America, and he used British sea power to stop French supplies and troops from reaching Canada. He also improved the relationship with the American colonies by treating them with respect and taking better advantage of their militias. He asked for their help to invade Canada and carry "the War into the Heart of the Enemy's Possessions."

Victories

During a previous war, the British had captured and then returned the French fortress at Louisbourg, which guarded

After years of defeats, British forces launched a series of successful attacks against French territory in the Ohio Valley and Canada.

the entrance to the St. Lawrence River and protected the heart of Canada. If the British could take Louisbourg again, they might be able to control Canada as well.

After several unsuccessful efforts, the British managed to capture Louisbourg in 1758 after a six-week siege. Its French-Canadian residents were forced to leave their homes and return to France. The British also took Fort Frontenac on Lake Ontario in August. These victories disrupted the French supply lines to their forts on the Great Lakes and in the Ohio Valley.

After more defeats, the French abandoned Fort Duquesne, and the British took control of the forks of the Ohio. They renamed the settlement Pittsburgh in honor of Prime Minister Pitt, and the city still goes by that name today.

The Iroquois nations had stayed neutral in the war so far. However, British victories and the persuasiveness of Sir William Johnson now led them to join the English side. With their help, the British managed to take Fort Niagara at the mouth of the

The Proclamation of 1763

When the French and Indian War ended, the British knew that peace with France did not guarantee peace with their Native American allies, especially if their colonists moved west onto tribal lands.

For England, the answer was simple: establish a border between British territory and Native American land. Settlers would not be allowed to move west, and anyone already living there would have to move back.

That October, England passed the **Proclamation** of 1763. It read in part:

> And whereas it is just and reasonable, and essential to our Interest, and the Security of our Colonies, that the several Nations or Tribes of Indians with whom We are connected, and who live under our Protection, should not be molested or disturbed in the Possession of such Parts of Our Dominions and Territories as … are reserved to them … as their Hunting Grounds.—We do therefore … strictly forbid, on Pain of our Displeasure, all our loving Subjects from making any Purchases or Settlements whatever, or taking Possession of any of the Lands above reserved.
>
> And We do further strictly enjoin and require all Persons whatever who have either

> wilfully or inadvertently seated themselves upon any Lands within the Countries above described … forthwith to remove themselves from such Settlements.

The English colonies vehemently disagreed with the idea that Great Britain could command them not to move west. They felt that their soldiers had fought for this land and now they should be rewarded. And, if colonists had already settled there, it would be terribly unjust to uproot them from their homes and move them back east.

The bigger issue was that colonists also resented that a government based thousands of miles away thought that it could dictate where and how they lived. Only a few years later, the Declaration of Independence criticized King George III for "raising the conditions of new appropriations of lands."

Great Britain's capture of Quebec signaled the end of French power in North America. Both commanding generals lost their lives during the fierce battle.

Niagara River on Lake Ontario in July 1759. This prevented French forts on the Great Lakes from getting supplies and reinforcements from Canada and led to their captures as well.

Canada Invasion

In 1759, the British attacked the key French location of Fort Carillon on Lake Champlain. They had tried before and had been defeated, including a particularly bloody attempt in 1758. This time, the French retreated in the face of the British advance. The British renamed their new prize Fort Ticonderoga. By controlling Lake Champlain, the British had now opened another path into Canada.

That summer, a huge British fleet headed up the St. Lawrence River toward the French stronghold of Quebec, which sat on a high bluff overlooking the river and featured tall defensive walls as well. James Wolfe commanded the British forces, while General Montcalm commanded the French.

After spending three months looking for weaknesses in the French defenses, the British discovered a narrow path that led up the bluffs from the river to the city. The path was not well defended, and Wolfe managed to move his army up to a flat piece of land known as the Plains of Abraham, located just outside Quebec's walls. Montcalm decided to leave the city and attack the British lines before they had the chance to organize a siege.

After a fierce battle, the British took Quebec on September 18, and the remaining French forces retreated toward Montreal. Both Wolfe and Montcalm died from wounds suffered during the battle.

British Victory

For all intents and purposes, the loss of Quebec signaled the end of French power in North America. The British proceeded to take Montreal and then Detroit as well as other French cities and forts.

Exhausted by worldwide war, Great Britain and France finally signed the Treaty of Paris in 1763. According to the terms of the treaty, France gave up all its claims to territory in Canada as well as India. France had already ceded its possessions in Louisiana to Spain in a separate agreement in 1762.

Spain had lost Cuba to the English during the war. The terms of the treaty returned Cuba to Spain while, in exchange, Spain gave Florida to England.

After The War: New Problems

The Treaty of Paris ended the French and Indian War and removed the French from all their territory in North America.

While the British won the war, however, they now had another tough job: they had to rule, defend, and manage the lands they controlled. As it turned out, that job was much bigger and more difficult than the British could ever have expected.

CHAPTER FOUR

Steps Toward Independence

In the late 1800s, an American historian named Francis Parkman wrote a seven-volume study about the struggle between the English and the French in North America. When France signed the Treaty of Paris, Parkman wrote, "half a continent … changed hands at the scratch of a pen."

That may seem hard to believe, but it is true. The Treaty of Paris forever changed the landscape of North America. France gave up all of its territory on the continent and transferred over to Great Britain far more land than the British had before, including Canada and the Ohio country.

Keep Canada?

While the terms of the treaty were being negotiated, some officials in Great Britain spoke against taking Canada from the French. They thought it would be better to hold on to islands like Guadeloupe in the West Indies that produced valuable products like sugar, as well as fishing rights in the north Atlantic, instead of giving those back to the French.

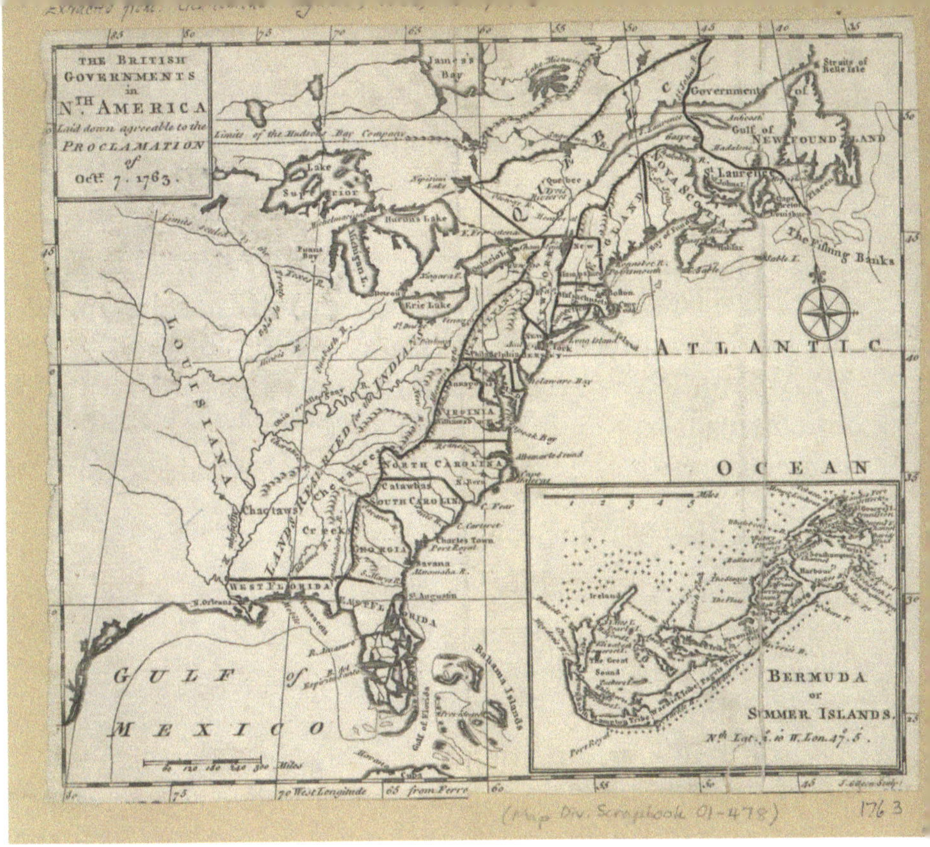

The Proclamation of 1763 angered English colonists by prohibiting settlers from moving west into protected Native American lands.

Others disagreed. Long before television or the internet existed, people wrote down their opinions and circulated them in newspapers and **pamphlets**. Some writers pleaded for England to take Canada from the French. "You must keep Canada, otherwise you lay the foundation for another war" said one. Another wrote, "If we do not exclude the [French] absolutely and entirely from that country we shall soon find we have done nothing."

Unexpected Consequences

As it turned out, the addition of Canada to the existing colonies strained British resources. They had beaten the French, but the English now had to manage and protect these new lands in addition to the colonies they already had. Some

French traders and settlers still lived there as well, so England had to consider their needs.

England also had to decide how to deal with Native Americans in the area. Many colonists bitterly resented the tribes that fought with the French and cruelly attacked English villages. For their part, Native Americans mistrusted the English, especially when it came to controlling the land.

As it turned out, some of the decisions that Great Britain made to handle these issues backfired, leading to consequences that the British could never have imagined.

A Good Beginning

Things did not start off badly. When the war ended, colonists were relieved that the fighting was over and the French were gone. They were also grateful to England, their mother country, for its help.

Benjamin Franklin summarized these feelings when he wrote a letter to the British government in January of 1760 after the victory in Canada:

> No one can rejoice more sincerely than I do on the Reduction [defeat] of Canada; and this, not merely as I am a Colonist, but as I am a Briton. I have long been of Opinion that the Foundations of the future Grandeur and Stability of the British Empire lie in America.

However, the situation quickly worsened.

Costs and Debt

Great Britain won the war over France in both North America and Europe, but wars cost a lot of money. The government had borrowed heavily to finance the war, and now it was time to pay back the **debt**.

England believed that it fought the French and Indian War to protect the American colonies and to open up

Benjamin Franklin and other colonial leaders turned against Britain after it increased taxes and passed laws they thought were unfair.

additional land for their expansion. The English government now thought it made perfect sense to collect money from the American colonies to pay its bills and also to reap the rewards of a larger empire.

The *Annual Register*, a yearly record of British and world events that began publishing in 1758, declared that the new territory "made our American empire [complete]. No frontiers could be more distinctly desired, nor more perfectly secured." The challenge now was to develop "an immense waste of savage country."

Growing Independence

While Great Britain still looked at the American colonies as its possessions, the colonists began to see things differently. During the early years of colonization, British settlers depended on their home government for protection against French, Spanish, and Native American attacks, as well as for goods and services they needed to survive.

Over the years, however, the colonies had become well established and better capable of supporting themselves. Royal governors still represented the king in each colony, but they often let colonial **legislatures** handle day-to-day affairs with little interference. This system had existed for nearly one hundred years.

Now the French had been defeated, so the colonies felt safer and more secure. They thought it simply wasn't fair that Great Britain was now trying to collect more money and exerting even more control over colonial affairs than in the past.

In addition to colonial anger, the British government faced another big problem.

Native American Mistrust

Many tribes loyal to the French were caught by surprise when the French lost the war and England took control of French territory. Some tribes assumed that they could get the same treatment from the English as they had from the French, including supplies and trade as well as protection from their enemies.

But Lord Amherst, who was now in charge of North America, ordered Native Americans to leave the former French forts and settlements. He also stopped giving them food and ammunition that they had come to depend on. Even worse, English colonists began to move west into the Ohio River country.

Ottawa Chief Pontiac led a Native American rebellion against British control in the Great Lakes region. The fighting lasted for three years.

These new settlers behaved very differently than the French. They wanted to build farms and towns, and they had no real desire to coexist with the Native Americans who had lived there for many years. New and larger English settlements made it difficult for the Native Americans to hunt and trade as they had before.

Pontiac's Rebellion

In May of 1763, the Ottawa chief Pontiac, once a strong ally of the French, led a rebellion of Native Americans against British rule in the former French territories along the western frontier. He was inspired by a Native American holy man, Neolin, who claimed to have had a vision that called for all Native American nations to reject their dependence on Europeans. Neolin wanted his people to return to their traditional life and diet and stop using European goods.

Referring to the red coats of the British army, Pontiac told his people that:

> These dogs dressed in red, who have come to rob you of your hunting-grounds and drive away the game—you must lift the hatchet against them. Wipe them from the face of the earth, and then you will win my favor back again, and once more be happy and prosperous.

Proclamation of 1763

Pontiac's rebellion represented just one in a series of violent episodes between English colonists and Native Americans after the French and Indian War ended. To prevent further bloodshed, Great Britain developed what it thought would be a good solution. It would simply stop colonists from moving west into Native American territory, and it would force any colonists already living there to move back east.

That October, King George III issued the Proclamation of 1763. This act (see sidebar in chapter 3) banned settlers from moving west of the Appalachian Mountains and designated the land between the mountains and the Mississippi River as a Native American reserve.

None Happy

George Washington was among the colonists who felt that the Proclamation of 1763 was only meant as "a temporary expedient to quiet the minds of the Indians." However, a majority of the colonists resented the proclamation and refused to obey it. Native Americans also rejected it; the British had already violated the terms of earlier treaties, and the tribes did not trust the British to act any differently with this new rule.

After three years of warfare, Chief Pontiac finally gave up his rebellion in 1766. Unfortunately, the fighting between white settlers and Native American tribes would continue for more than another century. In the end, most Native American tribes in

From Briton to Revolutionary

No person better symbolizes the changes that took place in North America during and after the French and Indian War than George Washington.

He was a loyal British subject who had fought with the Virginia militia during the French and Indian War. Then he suffered the consequences of British economic policy. Britain controlled the price of the tobacco Washington grew on his farm in Virginia. It also marked up the price of the many goods he bought from England. He was soon in debt.

George Washington turned against England.

Washington was unable to farm his way out of debt. The Proclamation of 1763 granted land in the Ohio Valley to veterans of the French and Indian War, but it also restricted British settlement in the region. Washington believed that land in the Ohio Valley would solve his financial woes. With Britain about to open some land in the Ohio Valley for settlement, Washington in 1767 petitioned for 200,000 acres owed to him and his soldiers. However, in 1774, Lord Hillsborough declared that land would go only to British regulars and not to Americans. Washington had been denied a commission in the British military so he didn't receive any land.

The final straw for Washington was seeing the mother country pass unfair taxes and attack New England colonists. He also felt that Americans would be left out of any westward expansion. Therefore, he accepted an invitation to lead the Continental Army and then served the new nation as the first President of the United States.

the United States were forced to move far from their homelands to reservations in western states such as Oklahoma. Many of these reservations still exist today and have their own sad history.

Economic Oppression

The British had always passed laws restricting the economic freedom of the colonists. After all, the reason the colonies existed was to make money for the mother country. The idea then was that colonies would send raw materials to Britain, where they would be made into goods. The English would then sell those goods back to the colonies. This would increase the nation's balance of trade and therefore its wealth.

In the 1660s, Parliament passed the Navigation Acts. These acts said certain goods, including tobacco and cotton, could only be shipped from the colonies on British ships. Also, all manufactured goods had to be sent from England to the colonies on British ships. The effect of the Navigation Acts was to slow the growth and restrict the freedom of the American economy. In 1720, the British quietly decided to reduce their efforts to enforce these acts.

Things changed after the French and Indian War. The Proclamation of 1763 was not the only regulation the British tried to impose on the American colonies. Desperate for money and to assert control, the English government also passed a series of laws, or acts, that affected colonial life.

In the past, each colony had its own legislature, and those legislatures levied taxes to raise the money needed to run the colonies. Now the British started charging their own fees to the colonies. They also returned to enforcing the Navigation Acts.

In 1763, Great Britain passed the Sugar Act, which collected taxes on sugar and molasses in the American colonies. Two years later, Great Britain passed the Stamp Act. Every official government document, as well as other publications like newspapers and even playing cards, had to be printed on paper embossed with an official stamp.

Excitement over Stamp Act.

Angry mobs took to the streets to protest British laws like the Stamp Act. Colonists would soon take up arms against Britain.

In 1765, the British government also passed the Quartering Act, which gave the British Army the power to base soldiers in buildings and use services in the colonies at no or little cost. Two years after that, Parliament passed the Townshend Acts, which included duties on lead, paper, glass, paint, and tea.

The colonists thought that, since they could not vote in British elections, the British government should not have the right to tax them. "No taxation without representation" became a popular saying.

Colonies Not United

As colonists began to disagree with British policies, they argued among themselves about how to respond. Some leaders like Samuel Adams in Boston wanted to resist and entirely rid the country of British authority. Others, like Benjamin Franklin in Pennsylvania and George Washington from Virginia, wanted to try to convince England to change its positions.

Noting that disputes now existed among English countrymen so soon after the end of the French and Indian War, the Reverend Samuel Johnson of Connecticut wrote in December 1763:

> It is truly a miserable thing that we no sooner leave fighting our neighbours, the French, but we must fall to quarrelling among ourselves.

Protests spread throughout the colonies, with more people calling for armed resistance against the British. Only a few years after the British and their American subjects had united to defeat the French and their Native American allies, the two sides now engaged in bitter debate about who would rule these new, expanded American lands.

In 1770, British troops at the Customs House in Boston fired on a crowd that had assembled to protest British taxes, killing five colonists. This is known as the Boston Massacre. In April 1775, the first shots of the American Revolution were fired at Lexington and Concord in Massachusetts.

Full Circle

The French and Indian War began as a battle between two European powers for supremacy in North America. In 1763, Britain's victory removed France, but it also led to divisions between the English government and its colonies in America. In 1778, France gained a measure of revenge against its longtime enemy, England, and recognized the American colonies as a sovereign nation.

With France's help, America finally won its independence, and the United States was born.

Chronology

Dates in green pertain to events discussed in this volume.

April 10, 1606: King James I issues the First Virginia Charter to the Virginia Company, authorizing its leaders to establish the Virginia colony and beginning the Colonial period.

May 13, 1607: The first permanent English colony in the New World is established at Jamestown, Virginia.

July 30, 1619: The House of Burgesses, the first legislative assembly in the colonies, convenes.

September 6, 1620: The *Mayflower* leaves Plymouth, England, for North America.

November 9, 1620: The Pilgrims see land for the first time on their trip; it is Cape Cod.

November 11, 1620: Adult males on the *Mayflower* sign the Mayflower Compact.

December 21, 1620: The Pilgrims land in Plymouth, Massachusetts.

Fall 1621: The Pilgrims and the Wampanoag celebrate a fall harvest festival together in what is considered the first Thanksgiving celebration in America.

May 1624: The Dutch establish the colony of New Netherland.

March 4, 1629: The Massachusetts Bay Company receives a charter from Charles I to trade in New England; the company's Puritan leaders land at Salem on June 12, 1630.

1632: Charles I grants to Lord Baltimore territory north of the Potomac, which becomes Maryland; the king does not restrict residency to Protestants, so Catholics are allowed.

March 3, 1634: The *Ark* and the *Dove* sail up the Chesapeake Bay, carrying the first settlers of Maryland; on March 25, the group purchases land from the Natives and names their settlement St. Mary's.

June 1636: Roger Williams founds the colony of Rhode Island.

September 7, 1664: The Dutch surrender New Amsterdam to the English, who rename the colony New York.

June 24, 1675: The Native population attacks Swansea,

Massachusetts, at the start of an attempt to wipe out the English settlers with a massive military action. This starts King Philip's War.

August 12, 1676: King Philip's War ends.

March 4, 1681: Charles II grants William Penn a charter for what becomes Pennsylvania.

May 1689: King William's War, the first French and Indian War, begins with the British declaring war on France; the war ends in 1697 with the Treaty of Ryswick.

October 7, 1691: The Province of Massachusetts Bay is chartered, merging the Massachusetts Bay Colony with the Maine and Plymouth territories to form a larger colony.

June 8, 1692: The Plymouth General Council has its last meeting.

May 4, 1702: Queen Anne's War, the second French and Indian War, begins; it ends in 1713 with France ceding Newfoundland and Nova Scotia to Britain.

February 29, 1704: French and Indian forces kill fifty residents and take more than one hundred captives in a raid on Deerfield, Massachusetts.

September 22, 1711: The Tuscarora Indian War begins in North Carolina; surviving Native Americans move north to New York to join the League of Six Nations.

April 21, 1732: King George signs a charter creating Georgia and establishes a board of trustees to govern the colony.

April 3, 1735: Britain ratifies an act banning slavery in Georgia.

May 28, 1754: Troops representing France and Great Britain and their Native Americans allies battle at Fort Duquesne in a struggle for control of the Ohio River Valley. This is the first fighting in what becomes the Seven Years' War, otherwise known and the French and Indian War.

July 3, 1754: George Washington surrenders Fort Necessity to the French.

July 9, 1755: General Braddock and the British are defeated at the Battle of the Wilderness; Braddock dies of wounds received in that battle four days later.

September 9, 1755: British Colonel William Johnson's forces win the Battle of Lake George, making Johnson the first British hero of the war.

May 15, 1756: Britain declares war on France, officially starting the French and Indian War. This start date is why the conflict is called the Seven Years' War in Europe.

August 8, 1757: British Fort Henry surrenders to the French under General Louis-Joseph de Montcalm-Grozon. Native Americans massacre many prisoners in an action later dramatized in James Fenimore Cooper's *The Last of the Mohicans.*

July 26, 1758: The British take Louisbourg, Nova Scotia and destroy the French fleet that was protecting Canada.

November 26, 1758: The British recapture Fort Duquesne. It is renamed "Pittsburgh."

July 26, 1759: The British capture Fort Niagara after the French abandon Fort Carillon (Ticonderoga).

September 13, 1759: British forces capture Quebec City in the climactic battle of the French and Indian War; the leaders of both armies, General Montcalm of the French and Commander James Wolfe of the British, die in the fighting.

September 8, 1760: Montreal and all of New France surrender to British commander Jeffery Amherst. The surrender of Montreal marks the end of the French and Indian War in North America.

August 15, 1761: French and Spanish kings sign the Bourbon Family compact; Spain enters the war as a French ally in November.

February 10, 1763: The signing of the Treaty of Paris ends the French and Indian War. This closes the Colonial period.

May 9, 1763: Pontiac's War begins with an attack on British fort at Detroit.

October 7, 1763: King George III issues the Proclamation of 1763.

Glossary

alliance An agreement between nations or groups of people promising mutual support.

confederacy A union of people or states that join together for a specific purpose.

debt Something that is owed, such as money or service.

guerrilla warfare A different way of fighting based on quick, sneak attacks and ambushes rather than massive, organized troop assaults.

indigenous Already existing in a place or country.

legislatures People who make or change laws and regulations in a state or country.

massacre The killing of a large number of defenseless people.

militia Fighting forces made up of ordinary citizens, instead of professional soldiers, who remain at home until an emergency when they are called on to fight.

neutral Refusing to pick sides in a war or argument.

pamphlets Small booklets (even one page) that contain information or arguments for a particular subject.

Parliament Great Britain's elected legislature, it is similar to the US Congress.

pelts An animal's skin, including its fur.

prime minister The chief minister or a ruler of a state. In Britain, the leader of the parliamentary government.

proclamation A government declaration that sets new rules or policies.

scalping A cruel practice of cutting away a circle of skin, including the hair, from a victim during warfare to keep as a trophy and to prove that a warrior has killed an opponent.

siege A military blockade of a city to keep out supplies to force those inside the city to surrender.

stockade A barrier of wooden stakes driven into the ground side by side to make an enclosure, used for defense against attack.

surveyor A person who measures the size, shape, or boundaries of pieces of land.

tactics A planned way of doing something.

tomahawks Small axes used as weapons.

Further Information

Books

Anderson, Fred. *The War That Made America: A Short History of the French and Indian War.* New York, NY: Viking Penguin, 2005.

Cooper, James Fenimore. *The Last of The Mohicans: A Narrative of 1757.* New York, NY: Atheneum Books for Young Readers, reissue edition, 2013.

Nester, William R. *The French and Indian War and the Conquest of New France.* Norman, OK: University of Oklahoma Press, 2014.

Pederson, Charles E. *The French & Indian War* (Essential Events). Edina, MN: ABDO Publishing Company, 2010.

Preston, David L. *Braddock's Defeat: The Battle of the Monongahela and the Road to Revolution.* New York, NY: Oxford University Press, 2015.

Websites

George Washington's Mount Vernon: French and Indian War

http://www.mountvernon.org/george-washington/french-indian-war

This website is dedicated to George Washington's life and his home at Mount Vernon. The section on the French and Indian War contains information about Washington's involvement, maps of the times, and copies of Washington's own journals, videos, and expert interviews.

Perspectives on the French and Indian War: Primary Source Set

https://dp.la/primary-source-sets/sets/perspectives-on-the-french-and-indian-war

Produced by the Digital Public Library of America, this website includes a collection of documents, images and maps from the time of the French and Indian War. By analyzing, exploring, and interpreting these primary sources, students can gain insight into the experiences of the people who lived during that time and experienced eighteenth-century warfare.

The War That Made America

http://www.thewarthatmadeamerica.org/index_21.php

This website is dedicated to the PBS series about the French and Indian War. It includes biographies of key figures, historical notes, maps, suggestions for further reading, and links to other sites.

DVDs

***The Last of the Mohicans*. Beverly Hills, CA. Michael Mann. 2010. (Blu-ray DVD)**

This 1992 movie is based on the 1826 novel by James Fenimore Cooper. While some historical details may be inaccurate, the movie portrays the harsh conditions that armies, colonists, and Native Americans faced during the time of the French and Indian War.

Bibliography

Books

Borneman, Walter R. *The French And Indian War: Deciding the Fate of North America.* New York, NY: HarperCollins Publishers, 2006.

Calloway, Colin G. *The Scratch of a Pen: 1763 and the Transformation of North America.* New York, NY: Oxford University Press, 2006.

Clary, David A. *George Washington's First War: His Early Military Adventures.* New York, NY: Simon & Schuster, 2011.

Fowler, William M. Jr. *Empires at War: The French and Indian War and the Struggle for North America, 1754-1763.* New York, NY: Walker & Company, 2005.

Hakim, Joy. *From Colonies to Country (A History of US: Book Three).* New York, NY: Oxford University Press, 2003.

Maestro, Betsy. *Struggle for a Continent: The French and Indian Wars, 1689-1763.* New York, NY: HarperCollins Publishers, 2000.

Russell, Francis. *The French and Indian Wars.* New York, NY: American Heritage Publishing Co, Inc., 1962.

Santella, Andrew. *The French and Indian War (We the People).* Minneapolis, MN: Compass Point Books: 2004.

Schwartz, Seymour I. *The French and Indian War 1754-1763: The Imperial Struggle for North America.* New York, NY: Simon & Schuster, 1994.

Strum, Richard M. *Causes of the American Revolution (Road to War)*. Stockton, NJ: OTTN Publishing, 2005.

Online Articles

"Algonquin Indian Fact Sheet." Native Languages of the Americas. Accessed March 31, 2017. http://www.bigorrin.org/algonquin_kids.htm

Bray, George A. III. "Scalping During the French and Indian War." Varsity Tutors. Accessed March 26, 2017. https://www.varsitytutors.com/earlyamerica/early-america-review/volume-3/scalping-during-the-french-and-indian-war

"Dutch Colonies." National Park Service. Accessed March 31, 2017. https://www.nps.gov/nr/travel/kingston/colonization.htm

"Excerpts From Speeches by Canassatego, an Iroquois, as Printed by Benjamin Franklin, 1740s." Smithsonian Source. Accessed April 4, 2017. http://www.smithsoniansource.org/display/primarysource/viewdetails.aspx?TopicId=&PrimarySourceId=1195

"French and Dutch Exploration in the New World." Khan Academy. Accessed March 31, 2017. https://www.khanacademy.org/humanities/us-history/colonial-america/early-english-settlement/a/french-and-dutch-exploration

"French and Indian War." History.com. Accessed March 29, 2017.http://www.history.com/topics/french-and-indian-war

"French and Indian War: North American History." Encyclopædia Britannica, March 17, 2015. https://www.britannica.com/event/French-and-Indian-War

"French and Indian War/Seven Years' War, 1754–63 (Milestones: 1750–1775)." Office of the Historian, US Department of State. Accessed March 27, 2017. https://history.state.gov/milestones/1750-1775/french-indian-war

"The French and Indian War (1754–1763): Timeline." Spark Notes. Accessed March 29, 2017. http://www.sparknotes.com/history/american/frenchindian/timeline.html

"George Washington Biography." Biography.com. Accessed April 7, 2017. http://www.biography.com/people/george-washington-9524786

Greenspan, Jesse. "Remembering the Proclamation of 1763." History.com, October 7, 2013. http://www.history.com/news/remembering-the-proclamation-of-1763

Howard, Ella and James Walsh. "Perspectives on the French and Indian War: Primary Source Set." Digital Public Library of America. Accessed March 29, 2017. https://dp.la/primary-source-sets/sets/perspectives-on-the-french-and-indian-war

"Making the Revolution: America 1763-1791." America In Class. Accessed March 24, 2017. http://americainclass.org/sources/makingrevolution/crisis/text1/text1.htm

"Mary Jemison Recalling, in 1824, Her Capture by Indians during the French and Indian War: Primary Sources." Smithsonian Source. Accessed March 28, 2017. http://www.smithsoniansource.org/display/primarysource/viewdetails.aspx?TopicId=&PrimarySourceId=1197

"Original Document: Letter from Virginia's Governor Dinwiddie to the French Commander in the Ohio Country, October, 1753." Explore PA History. Accessed March 26, 2017. http://explorepahistory.com/odocument.php?docId=1-4-1A

Raphael, Ray. "Why Did George Washington Become a Revolutionary." Journal of the American Revolution, February 16, 2015. https://allthingsliberty.com/2015/02/why-did-george-washington-become-a-revolutionary

"The Royal Proclamation of 1763." US History. Accessed April 7, 2017. http://www.ushistory.org/us/9a.asp

"Sir William Johnson, 1715–1774, Papers, 1738–1808." New York State Library. Accessed March 31, 2017. http://www.nysl.nysed.gov/msscfa/sc7005.htm

"Unit 1—Spain in the New World to 1600." National Park Service. Accessed March 31, 2017. https://www.nps.gov/fora/learn/education/unit-1-spain-in-the-new-world-to-1600.htm

Index

Page numbers in **boldface** are illustrations. Entries in **boldface** are glossary terms.

About the Author

GERRY BOEHME is a published author, editor, speaker, and business consultant who was born in New York City. He loves to travel and to learn about new things. He especially enjoys talking with people who have different backgrounds and opinions.

Gerry has written books for students dealing with many subjects, including *Edward Snowden: Heroic Whistleblower or Traitorous Spy*, *John Lewis and Desegregation*, *Heresy: The Spanish Inquisition (Public Persecutions)* and *Roberto Clemente: The Pride of Puerto Rico*. He has also published many articles dealing with media, advertising and new technology, and he has been featured as a speaker at business conferences across the United States as well as the United Kingdom, Australia, and the Republic of Korea.

Gerry graduated from the Newhouse School at Syracuse University and now lives on Long Island, New York with his wife and two children.